# Monkey
# Me
### AND THE
### Golden Monkey

### BY
## TIMOTHY ROLAND

## BRANCHES™

### SCHOLASTIC INC.

Read all the **Monkey Me** books!

#1 — Monkey Me and the Golden Monkey — TIMOTHY ROLAND

#2 — Monkey Me and the Pet Show — TIMOTHY ROLAND

#3 — Monkey Me and the New Neighbor — TIMOTHY ROLAND

#4 — Monkey Me and the School Ghost — TIMOTHY ROLAND

# Table of Contents

## To Mom and Dad
## –T.R.

Library of Congress Cataloging-in-Publication Data Available

ISBN 978-0-545-55977-5 (hardcover) / ISBN 978-0-545-55976-8 (paperback)

12 11 10 9 8 7 6 5 4 3 2 1          14 15 16 17 18 19/0

Printed in China          38
First Scholastic printing, January 2014

Book design by Liz Herzog

## Chapter 1
# Keep Moving!

"Stop!" my teacher, Miss Plum, said. "It might not be safe!"

I kept reaching for the banana.

"Clyde!" Miss Plum knocked my hand away. "Were you listening?"

I nodded.

But I wasn't.

Well, I did hear a little.

Dr. Wally, a scientist, told my class he had blasted the bowl of fruit with a special ray. He hoped the fruit would grow super large.

But it still looked normal.

"Isn't this interesting, class?" Miss Plum asked.

Everyone nodded.

Except me.

I was on a school field trip to the science museum.

I wanted to see dinosaur skeletons. And mummies. And the Golden Monkey!

But I was stuck in a back room listening to Dr. Wally talk about fruit.

I was bored and needed to move.

"Okay, class," Miss Plum said. "You have one hour to look around the rest of the museum before our bus leaves."

"Yippee!" I yelled.

"And no monkey business!" Miss Plum stared at me.

But I was already out of the back room and in the museum's main lobby.

My head started spinning. There was lots to see. Lots to do.

I had to keep moving.

"Slow down, Clyde!"

I turned and looked at Claudia, my twin sister. "You're getting too excited," she said. "And that means you're headed for trouble!"

"Me? Get in trouble? Ha!" I said.

"Well, I'm sticking with you to make sure you don't!" Claudia grabbed my arm.

I tried to break free, but couldn't. So I pulled my sister to the dinosaur room.

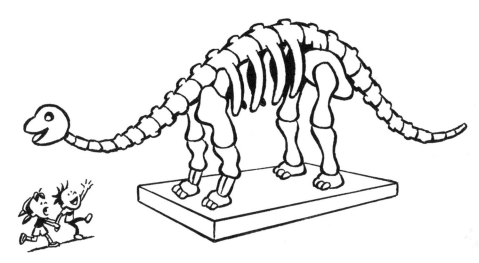

"Wow!" I reached toward a skeleton.

Claudia pulled me back. "Don't touch it, Clyde!"

"I wasn't planning to," I said.

"Good!" Claudia said.

"I was planning to climb it," I said. "Like monkey bars."

"You're kidding, aren't you?" Claudia's hand slipped off my arm.

"Ha!" I said. "See you later, alligator!"

Claudia tried to grab me again, but missed!

"Come back, Clyde!" she yelled.

I ran from my sister and into the hallway.
Then I pulled a Golden Monkey toy from my
pocket.

I had bought it at the museum's gift shop.
It was made of heavy plastic and was painted
gold.

It looked just
like the museum's
Golden Monkey,
which was made
of solid gold!

I ran even
faster.

I raced around a corner. I couldn't wait to see the real Golden Monkey!

I ran into the room where it was on display. Then . . .

## chapter 2
# Golden Monkeys

It felt like I had run into a truck.

I was on the floor. I saw stars around my head.

I looked at the museum guard next to me. He was big. Like a truck.

He pushed himself off the floor and looked around. But not at me.

"Sorry," I said.

The guard growled and kept looking.

I felt something poking me in the back. I rolled over and saw I was lying on two Golden Monkeys!

I picked mine up and stuck it in my pocket. At least, I thought it was mine. The two Golden Monkeys looked exactly alike.

Then I picked up the second one. "This must be yours," I said to the guard.

He grabbed the Golden Monkey from my hand. He looked at it and smiled. Then he looked at me and glared.

He was scary!

So I turned and ran.

Maybe the guard was still angry at me for bumping into him. All I knew was that I needed to get away.

I ran as fast as I could down the hall. I saw an open doorway. I raced inside and shut the door.

I was alone.

Safe.

But lost.

Or maybe not. In front of me was Dr. Wally's bowl of fruit.

My stomach growled.

I was hungry and stepped closer. "It looks safe to me," I said.

I grabbed the banana. I split the peel. I took a bite just as the door slammed open.

"Clyde!" Claudia ran into the room. "What are you doing?"

"Eating." I held out the banana. "Want some?"

"Are you crazy?" my sister asked.

"No," I said. "The banana's fine."

"Really?" Claudia asked.

I nodded and took another bite.

"Well, the bus is leaving. So come on, Clyde!" Claudia walked toward the door. "Or you'll get in trouble."

"Me? Get in trouble? Ha!" I stuffed the rest of the banana in my mouth.

It tasted yummy!

At first.

## chapter 3
# Feeling Super

"Are you feeling okay, Clyde?" Claudia asked.

"Why?" I asked.

"You're sitting still." Claudia laughed.

"Ha! Very funny!" I said. But I knew my sister was right. Like usual.

I was on the bus heading back to school. I usually have lots of energy. I usually bounce on the seat.

But my body felt heavy.

And sleepy.

I couldn't wait to get into class and take a nap.

"We're here!" Miss Plum said.

I stepped off of the bus and onto the playground. Then . . .

KA-POW!

Suddenly I was on the ground.

"Ha-ha! Squashed you!" Roz said.

I looked up at the class bully and groaned.

"Now fly away, little bug!" Roz said.

I stood and tried to run. But my legs wouldn't move.

"I said, scram!" Roz yelled as she gave me a shove.

My body wobbled.

I heard laughter around me.

Then Roz shoved me again. And again.

"Leave Clyde alone, Roz!" Claudia stepped in front of her.

Roz glared.

Claudia glared back.

Roz looked at me and laughed. "We'll finish this later, little bug!" she said.

I tried watching as she walked toward the school building. But it was hard to keep my eyes open.

"Are you okay, Clyde?" Claudia asked.

My head started spinning.

My stomach felt ready to explode.

My sister's face looked fuzzy. "I'm fine," I said.

"Come on, Clyde!" Claudia said. "We need to get to class!"

I don't remember walking there. All I know is everything turned black. Then I woke up sitting at my desk.

And the pain in my stomach was gone!

"Did you hear what I said, Clyde?" Miss Plum asked.

"Ah . . . no," I said.

Several of my classmates laughed.

"I said, be careful with the paste!" My teacher stared at me.

"The paste?" I whispered.

I scratched my head. I had no idea what was happening. But just then Miss Plum passed out yellow paper. And scissors.

"Yippee!" I yelled. "Art class!"

Miss Plum glared.

"Sorry," I said. But I couldn't stop smiling.

"I see you're feeling better now," Claudia whispered. She sits at the desk next to mine.

"I'm feeling super!" I bounced on my chair. "Art is my favorite class!"

"Calm down," Claudia said.

"I'm trying," I said. "But I can't!"

My head started spinning. My heart raced.

Faster.

And faster.

I sneezed.

"A-CHOO!"

I felt a wave of energy splash through me.

I had to move. So when Miss Plum wasn't looking, I ran into the hallway.

# chapter 4
# MonKey Me

## chapter 5
# This is Crazy!

I didn't wait for Claudia. When school was over, I ran home as fast as I could.

I was confused. Like usual.

But this time it wasn't a math problem I didn't understand.

It was a monkey problem!

I didn't know why I had turned into a real monkey! Or how.

"Clyde!" Claudia yelled. She followed me through the front door and upstairs.

"Leave me alone!" I said.

Claudia pulled me into her bedroom. "What were you doing in the school hallway for so long during art class today, Clyde?"

She sat on her bed.

I looked around her room . . . at her books . . . at her model rockets . . . at her stuffed animals.

"So what happened?" Claudia asked.

"Nothing happened," I said.

"Miss Plum wasn't very happy with you, Clyde," Claudia said.

"What else is new?" I said.

Claudia stared at my face. "Something's wrong, isn't it?" she asked.

I didn't want to tell her.

But I knew my sister would bug me until I did. I also knew that maybe she could help me figure out why it happened.

I was the twin full of energy. Claudia was the twin full of brains.

"Okay, here goes," I said. "I turned into a monkey and played in the school hallway. Then I turned back into a boy."

"That's the craziest story I've ever heard!" Claudia said.

"But it happened!" I said.

"Ha-ha! Very funny, Clyde!" My sister looked at me like I had imagined the whole thing.

She didn't believe I had

turned into a monkey. Now I wasn't sure I believed it, either.

I felt silly.

I felt like I had to move!

I dashed over and grabbed a bunny stuffed animal from my sister's bookshelf.

"So what really happened in the school hallway today, Clyde?" Claudia asked.

I tossed the bunny into Claudia's trash basket. "He scores!" I yelled as a wave of energy splashed through me.

I bounced. I laughed. I grabbed the bunny and shot again.

"Calm down, Clyde!" Claudia said.

"I can't," I said.

My head started spinning. My heart raced
Faster. And faster.

I sneezed. "A-CHOO!"

I fell behind my sister's bed.

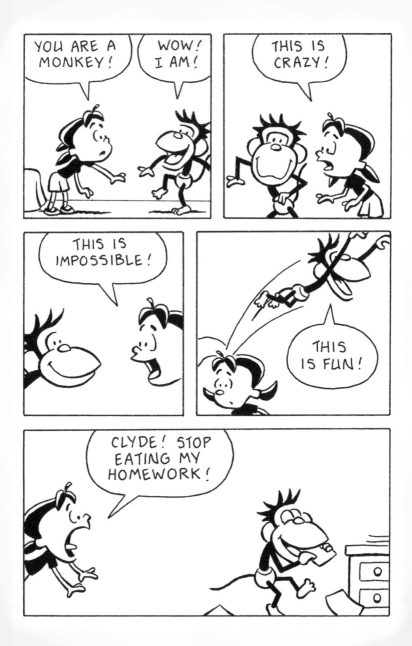

## chapter 6
# What Happened?

"Amazing!" Claudia said.

I looked and saw I was human again. No monkey hair. Or ears. Or tail.

"How did you do that?" Claudia asked.

"I don't know," I said.

"And how do you feel?" she asked.

"I feel . . . hungry," I said.

Claudia looked at me and giggled.

"What's so funny?" I asked. "I need to eat."

"But first, Clyde, you need to put your clothes on." Claudia giggled louder.

I jumped behind her bed. I had forgotten I was in my sister's room wearing nothing but my underpants!

I quickly dressed.

"From now on I'm wearing shorts under my long pants," I said. "In case I turn into a monkey again."

"But why did it happen?" Claudia asked.

"Maybe it's because I like monkeys so much," I said. I pulled my Golden Monkey from my pocket and smiled.

"You've always liked monkeys, Clyde," Claudia said. "But you've never turned into one before."

"Oh, right," I said.

"Although sometimes," Claudia said, "you act like one."

"Ha! Very funny, Claudia!" I walked to her bookshelf.

"Something must have happened in the last day or two that caused you to change into a monkey," Claudia said. "But what?"

I held my Golden Monkey on top of a model rocket. I waved the rocket in the air.

"Stop that, Clyde!" Claudia yelled.

"But monkeys fly in rockets," I said.

"Not in my rockets!" Claudia grabbed the model from me and set it back on her bookshelf.

I stuck the Golden Monkey back in my pocket.

"We need to figure out why you turned into a monkey, Clyde," Claudia said. "So stop fooling around and think!"

I sat next to my sister on her bed.

I thought about monkeys. I thought about turning into a monkey. I thought about how much fun it was to be a monkey.

"Stop bouncing, Clyde!" Claudia said.

"I'm not!" I said. But then I looked and saw that I was.

"Think, Clyde!" Claudia said.

"But I'm hungry." I headed toward the bedroom door. "I need a banana!"

"Wait!" Claudia ran after me. "That's it, Clyde!"

"What is?" I asked.

"The banana from Dr. Wally's experiment!" Claudia said. "The one you ate at the museum! Remember?"

 **40**

I remembered. "But what does that have to do with me turning into a monkey?" I asked.

"I don't know," Claudia said. "But we're going to find out."

She pulled me downstairs. I grabbed a banana and ate it. We told Mom we'd be back before supper.

Then we hopped on our bikes and rode quickly to the science museum.

## chapter 7
# Dr. Wally

We raced up the steps and into the science museum.

There was lots to see. Lots to do.

"Calm down!" Claudia grabbed my arm.

"I can't," I said.

"We're here to talk to Dr. Wally," Claudia said to me.

"Rats!" I said.

We walked to a back room. Dr. Wally was standing near a bowl of fruit.

"Welcome, children," he said when he saw us. "What can I do for you?"

"We were hoping you could help us," Claudia said.

"I'll try," Dr. Wally said. "But first, maybe you could help me find a banana."

"A banana?" I asked.

Dr. Wally pointed to the bowl of fruit. "It was here this morning."

"So were we." Claudia pushed me closer to Dr. Wally. "Tell him, Clyde!"

"I ate your banana," I said.

"Oh?" Dr. Wally looked at me closely. "And you're okay?"

"Yes," I said. "Except that I've turned into a monkey twice since I ate the banana."

"Hmm. Interesting!" Dr. Wally said.

"So why did it happen?" Claudia asked.

Dr. Wally thought for a moment.

"The banana was part of my experiment," he said. "It changed when I blasted it with the gamma ray. And Clyde's body changed when he ate the banana."

Dr. Wally looked at me again. "Clyde's inner monkey must now be able to grow big enough to become an outer monkey."

"What does that mean?" Claudia asked.

"When Clyde gets super excited," Dr. Wally said, "he will now not only act like a monkey, he will become one."

"Really?" Claudia looked worried.

Dr. Wally nodded.

"Isn't there a cure?" my sister asked.

"No. I mean . . . not yet," Dr. Wally said. "I'll try to find one. But it might take a while."

"Don't hurry," I said.

"Thanks for your help, Dr. Wally," Claudia said. Then she led me from the museum. "You turning into a monkey, Clyde, sounds like trouble."

"Me turning into a monkey," I said, "sounds like fun." I hopped on my bike and followed my twin sister home for supper.

## chapter 8
# Superstar

I woke up the next morning a little confused.

Did I really turn into a monkey the day before? Or was it just a dream?

I wasn't sure.

But I put shorts on under my long pants. Just in case it happened again.

I stuck my Golden Monkey in my pocket. I thought it might bring me luck.

I put an extra apple in my lunch bag to give to Miss Plum. "I want her to like me," I told Claudia as we walked to school.

"Then behave!" Claudia said.

We stepped onto the school playground. "I'll try," I said. The bell rang and I dashed toward the school building.

"Slow down, Clyde!" Claudia yelled.

I was already racing up the steps. I ran down the hall, into my classroom, and . . .

# KA-BUMP!

. . . into Miss Plum!

"Clyde!" she yelled.

"Sorry about that," I said.

My teacher helped me up.

"Am I in trouble?" I asked.

My teacher nodded.

I set the apple on her desk.

"You seem to always have lots of extra energy, Clyde," Miss Plum said. "And you must learn to use it to do something good."

"Like be a superhero?" I grinned.

Miss Plum rolled her eyes. Then she pointed to the small bulletin board.

"I need someone to decorate this board," she said. "Someone who likes art."

"I'll do it!" I said.

I think Miss Plum was trying to keep me busy and out of trouble. And it worked!

She wanted a springtime design. So during the early morning, I cut flowers out of colored paper.

I tacked them to the bulletin board. And some green paper grass. And a big yellow sun. And a bird in the sky.

"Class," Miss Plum said when I finished, "let's thank Clyde for his good work."

Then everyone clapped.

For me.

Like I was a hero.

And I bounced.

"Calm down, Clyde!" Claudia said.

"But I feel super!" I said.

Then my head started spinning. My heart raced. Faster. And faster.

I sneezed. "A-CHOO!"

I jumped up from my chair and ran into the hallway.

# chapter 9
# Monkey Speed

# chapter 10
# Me? Help?

"Come with me!" Principal Murphy said.

Claudia's face turned red. She had never been taken to the office before.

I had. Lots of times.

It meant I was in big trouble. And when I stepped into the office, I saw I was in big, BIG trouble!

The police chief was sitting behind the principal's desk. "Here's Clyde!" Principal Murphy pushed me toward him.

The police chief leaned closer. "The Golden Monkey was stolen from the museum yesterday," he said to me.

I gulped. "And you think I took it?"

"No," the police chief said. "But Principal Murphy said you run around a lot. So maybe you saw something yesterday at the museum that might help us catch the thief."

"Think, Clyde!" Principal Murphy said.

I tried. But it was hard to remember with everyone staring.

"Think, Clyde!" Claudia said.

"I can't!" I said as she grabbed my arm.

It reminded me of what she did at the museum. Before I ran from her. And crashed into the guard. And . . .

"Wait a minute!" I said. "I saw a guard with a Golden Monkey. But I thought it was a toy, like mine."

I felt the Golden Monkey in my pocket.

"Hmm. So the guard is the thief," the police chief said. "Do you remember what he looks like, Clyde?"

"Yes," I said. "I'll never forget his face."

The police chief showed me pictures on the computer of all the museum guards. But none of them looked like the thief.

"Are you sure?" the police chief asked.

"Yes," I said.

"Maybe Clyde is making up a story about seeing the guard," Principal Murphy said.

"Or maybe," Claudia said, "the guard wasn't really a guard."

"What?" everyone asked.

Claudia smiled. She is good at figuring things out. She is also good at trying to keep me out of trouble.

"Maybe the thief was dressed like a guard," she said.

"So he was in disguise," the police chief said, rubbing his chin. "That's how he escaped without being noticed."

"Except by me," I said. "And maybe I can help you catch the thief."

The police chief stood. "The thief has what he wants — the Golden Monkey," he said. "I doubt he'll be back."

"But you two better get back to your class," Principal Murphy said to Claudia and me.

I looked up at the clock. Then I hurried with my sister to our classroom.

## chapter **11**
# You're the Sub?

Nobody was in our classroom.

Claudia and I had missed lunch and most of recess.

I grabbed and quickly ate half a sandwich from my lunch bag.

I tried to think of what I should tell Miss Plum. I knew she wouldn't be happy I had run out of the classroom earlier.

The bell rang. Recess was over.

My classmates ran into the room. They sat at their desks.

I watched the doorway. But instead of Miss Plum, a big man with a mustache walked into the room.

"Miss Plum will not be back today," the man said. "So I will be your substitute teacher."

Several of my classmates grinned.

I usually get excited, too, when we have a sub. I like to play jokes on them.

But when the sub looked at me, my stomach felt sick.

"What's wrong, Clyde?" Claudia asked.

"I don't know," I said.

I thought I had seen the sub's face before. But not his dark curly hair. Or his thin curly mustache.

The sub picked up the class seating chart. "I need someone to help me carry boxes from the storage room to our classroom," he said.

Lots of hands shot up.

"How about Clyde?" He pointed at me.

My heart pounded. "But I didn't raise my hand," I said.

He pointed to the door. "Let's go!"

I slowly stood.

"Are you okay, Clyde?" Claudia asked.

I looked at my sister, but said nothing. I didn't have to. Her eyes told me she knew what I was thinking.

Something was wrong.

The sub looked at the seating chart again. "Claudia will be in charge while I am gone."

Then he gave me a little shove. "Let's get moving, Clyde!"

We walked out of the classroom. At the other end of the hall, he told me to stop.

"In here!" The sub opened a door. He pushed me into a room filled with boxes.

"Where is it, Clyde?" the sub asked.

"Where's what?" I asked.

"The Golden Monkey!" he said. He pulled off his wig and mustache.

"You're the guard . . . I mean, the thief!" I said.

He growled. "You mixed up our Golden Monkeys after crashing into me at the museum yesterday! You gave me your toy!"

"So I have the real one?" I asked.

"Yes," he said. "And I want it! NOW!"

The thief was big, looked mean, and was blocking the doorway. I had no other choice.

I pulled the real Golden Monkey from my pocket. He grabbed it from my hand. He stared at it and smiled.

"I'll be far away before you can get out of here and tell someone what happened," the thief told me.

Then he laughed. He stuck the real Golden Monkey in his pocket. He left the storage room and locked the door.

# chapter **12**
# Banana Pudding

"Miss Plum?" I quickly looked around the storage room. But all I saw were boxes.

"Are you okay, Clyde?" my teacher asked.

The voice came from a closet. "Yes, Miss Plum." I tried to open the closet door. But it had been locked with a key.

"A big man with a mustache tricked me," Miss Plum said. "He wanted me out of the classroom so he could get you."

"He tricked me, too," I said, "and brought me here to get the Golden Monkey."

I looked at the locked storage room door. I looked at the locked closet door.

I looked up and saw a ceiling vent. But it was too high to reach.

At least, too high for a boy.

But not too high for a monkey!

"It's time to change!" I told myself. "It's monkey time!" I closed my eyes and tried to think of something super exciting.

But nothing happened.

So I tried again.

But all I could think about was that my teacher was locked in the closet! And that I was locked in the storage room!

And that the thief was getting away with the Golden Monkey!

It made me angry. But just then I heard a voice coming from a speaker on the wall.

"There's been a change in today's lunch menu," it said.

"Sounds like Claudia," I said.

"Today's lunch dessert," the voice from the speaker said, "will now be ... banana pudding."

YUM! It was my favorite dessert!

Just thinking about eating a bowl of banana pudding made me smile.

Then my head started spinning. My heart raced. Faster. And faster.

I sneezed. "A-CHOO!"

## Chapter 13

# The Hero

BE CAREFUL, CLYDE!

I WILL.

I'LL BE BACK, MISS PLUM!

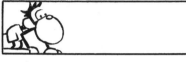

## chapter **14**
# Monkey Business

After school, Claudia and I rode our bikes to the science museum.

We hurried to the room where they kept the Golden Monkey.

It was back where it belonged!

Thanks to me.

Or rather, thanks to the monkey me.

"You did it, Clyde," Claudia said.

"And you helped, too," I said.

My sister didn't tell me how she had used the school's speaker system without getting caught. But I'm glad she did.

I bounced as I looked at the Golden Monkey. I was excited to see it. I was also excited about being in the museum.

"Calm down, Clyde!" Claudia said.

I looked around. "Why?" I asked.

Claudia grabbed my shoulder. "Because changing into a monkey makes you —"

"Special!" I said. "It's how I can use my extra energy to do something good. It's my superpower!"

"Oh, brother!" Claudia sighed.

"It's how I can help keep the world safe," I said. "Like I did by rescuing Miss Plum. And by catching the Golden Monkey thief."

I grinned. "And next time —"

"Next time?" Claudia's hand slipped off my shoulder.

"But first I have some unfinished business." I raced out of the Golden Monkey room. "Some unfinished monkey business," I said.

"Clyde!" Claudia chased after me.

I ran down the museum hallway. I slid around a corner.

My head started spinning. My heart raced. Faster. And faster.

I sneezed. "A-CHOO!"

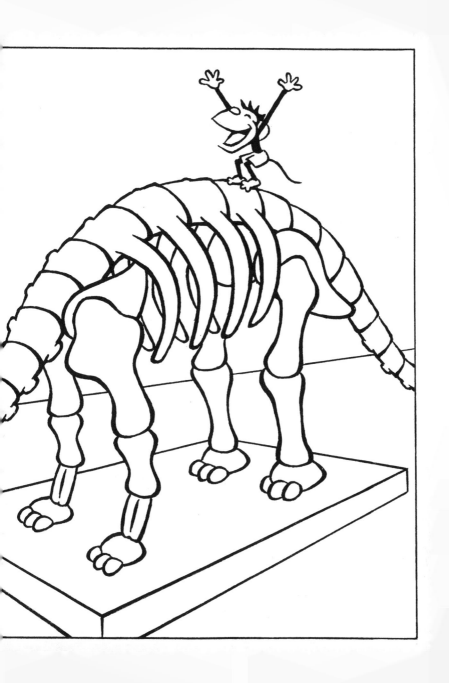

**Timothy Roland** likes monkeys, eating bananas, and telling stories. He has written and drawn pictures for over a dozen children's books, including the *Comic Guy* series for Scholastic.

Timothy lives and works in Pennsylvania. Like Clyde in this book, he sometimes acts like a monkey. But he has never turned into a real one. At least, not yet.

# Monkey Me

## QUESTIONS & ACTIVITES

### CAN YOU ANSWER THESE QUESTIONS ABOUT MONKEY ME AND THE GOLDEN MONKEY?

Verbs are action words. For example, when Clyde is a monkey he feels the need to **run**, **bounce**, and **jump**. What other verbs describe how monkeys move?

What two BIG things happen during Clyde's visit to the museum?

How does Claudia help Clyde stop the thief?

The thief appears on pages 10, 67, and 77. What is **different** and **the same** in these pictures?

Draw a comic strip. Show how Clyde turns into a monkey and show what he does when he is